To all of the hardworking teachers and librarians —especially Mrs. N. Murray and Mrs. M. Mullins, whose words directly inspired this story. And to Lola, who knew that Dragon needed a back -to-school story! — B.S.

For Nick x — S.H.

CLEVER
• Publishing •

Text copyright © 2021 by **Bianca Schulze**
Illustrations copyright © 2021 by **Samara Hardy**

First published in the United States of America in August 2021 by "Clever-Media-Group" LLC
www.clever-publishing.com
CLEVER is a registered trademark of "Clever-Media-Group" LLC

ISBN 978-1-951100-88-9 (hardcover)

For information about permission to reproduce selections from this book, write to:
CLEVER PUBLISHING
79 MADISON AVENUE; 8TH FLOOR
NEW YORK, NY 10016
USA

For general inquiries, contact: info@clever-publishing.com

To place an order for Clever Publishing books, please contact The Quarto Group:
sales@quarto.com • Tel: (+1) 800-328-0590

Art created with Procreate and Adobe Photoshop
Book design by Michelle Martinez

MANUFACTURED, PRINTED, AND ASSEMBLED IN CHINA
10 9 8 7 6 5 4 3 2 1

JUST BE Yourself DRAGON!

by

BIANCA SCHULZE

CLEVER
Publishing

illustrated by

SAMARA HARDY

Dragon?

Dragon?

Dragon?

Have you seen her lately?

Can you help me call for Dragon?

DRAAAAGOoONNN?

3

It's almost time for her first day of school, and I can't find her anywhere!

What's that you say?
She's under the bed?

4

She must be feeling a little nervous.
Can you tickle her tail to encourage
her to come out for breakfast?

That helped!

The castle cooks have made her a super-duper, scrumptious dragon breakfast. We don't want it to get cold.

Show Dragon how you sniff the air.

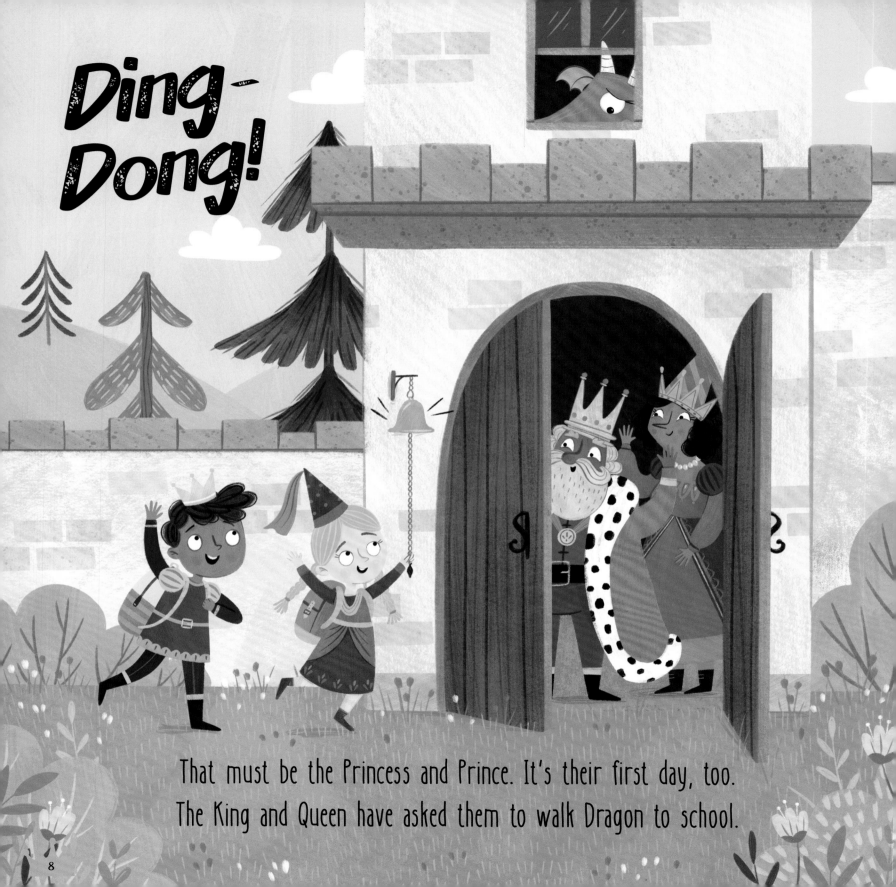

Ding-Dong!

That must be the Princess and Prince. It's their first day, too.
The King and Queen have asked them to walk Dragon to school.

Look! Is Dragon trying to hide?

Poor Dragon. I think she needs a friend to show her that school can be fun!

Raise your hand if you want to help her.

Let's all take a deep breath. **You've got this!**

We will be brave **together**.

JUST BE
Yourself
DRAGON!

VILLAGE
SCHOOL

CASTLE

11

At Village School, the day always begins with a cheery
"Good morning!" before Circle Time and a favorite story.

Oh, no!

Dragon might need someone to show her how to sit crisscross applesauce. It's a bit tricky for dragons.

Will you show her how to sit?

On Dragon's first day of school, there are so many new things to learn.

Color ratios

Weight distribution

Kinetic energy

$a = 2 + b^2$

Tail-eye coordination

Gravity

JUST BE *Yourself* DRAGON!

15

It's time for music class with the merry musicians.
Making quiet and loud sounds can be so much fun.

Let's chant:

whisper  whisper

whisper

whisper

Dragon accidentally breathed fire and burned the plant when she roared. Mistakes can happen even when we're having fun.

Let's give Dragon a reassuring pat.

Now might be a good
time for some lunch.

Thumbs up if you agree.

Hmm. The Princess and Prince aren't here yet.

Dragon doesn't know who to sit with.
Do you see any empty seats?

Yes!
Right here!

21

Dragon nervously walks over and asks the boy if he would like company. Dragon is brave and talks to him, even though she's nervous.

JUST BE Yourself DRAGON!

He said YES!

And the Princess and Prince join them, too.
Dragon is starting to look a lot more relaxed.

So relaxed that she accidentally knocks over the
milk! The Prince's sandwich is now all soggy.

Oh, no!

What's Dragon doing now?

Dragon huffs and puffs out fire—
and turns the sandwich into grilled cheese!

Wow! This tastes great!

How thoughtful, Dragon.
And all it took was
being herself.

Everyone lines up to talk to Dragon!

Rub your tummy if you'd like one of Dragon's grilled cheese sandwiches, too.

Now it's time for math class with a juggling jester!

Let's count along.

1, 2, 3...

Easy peasy!

4, 5, 6...

You've got this, Jester!

7, 8, 9...
Everyone feels nervous sometimes.

10!
Mistakes can happen even when we're having fun.

Oops!

At Village School, the day always ends the same way it began: with Circle Time and a favorite story.

Well . . . almost the same.
It looks like Dragon loved her day after all!

Nod your head if you agree.

I wonder how Dragon will feel about her second day of school?

JUST BE Yourself DRAGON!